HAUNTIQUES

WANDERING WAGON

written by Thomas Kingsley Troupe

illustrated by Rudy Faber

D1152291

raintree

a Capstone company — publishers for children

The screaming baseball smashes into the pocket of my glove, stinging my hand. Seeing my discomfort, Hai breaks into a big grin.

"Nice," I say.

It's Saturday. Hai and I have decided to give the video games a break. Actually, to be honest, my mum got sick of us sitting inside for hours. The weather has finally warmed to the point where we can play catch outside. Just little patches of dirty snow that have yet to melt are left.

I rocket one back his way. The ball goes wild, but Hai snags it before it whistles past.

"Mate," Hai says. "Get that arm under control, or it's going to be a long season."

"Yeah, yeah," I say. "Just warming up."

Near the patch of grass where we're playing catch, a bunch of kids run around a playground while their parents watch. The sun has coaxed all kinds of people out of their houses. Hai and I came here because our gardens are pretty small, and the area next to the playground offers more space. It doesn't hurt that I can see Days Gone Buy from where we're standing.

Days Gone Buy is an antique shop run by the new family in town, the Markles. Liz and Beth, twin sisters, are in the same year as Hai and me.

"So what's the story with Beth?" Hai asks.

"Not much of a story," I say, deftly snagging a fastball like we hadn't taken the winter off and skilfully avoiding the truth. I'm semi-secretly sort of crazy about Beth. "I see her at school, but we don't talk a whole lot."

"You're killing me, Casey," Hai says with a groan.

"What do you mean?" I say, trying to mask the emotion rising in my voice.

"It's obvious you like Beth," says Hai. "Those crazy twins moved in four months ago, and you haven't made a move."

"I know," I say, throwing the ball back and dropping my act. "But what am I supposed to say? Nice weather we're having? How's business at the shop?"

Hai catches my toss and shrugs. "I don't know," Hai says. "But something is better than nothing. I heard John Muffleman thinks Beth is cute."

I drop my arms. My baseball glove almost slips off of my hand. "Serious?" I ask. I search my best friend's expression to see if he's messing with me, because, let's face it, he usually is.

"Serious as a line drive to the face," Hai says, throwing the ball high in the air. "I heard him in PE on Thursday."

This is serious business. John Muffleman is one of the most popular guys at school. He's the captain of our baseball team, and his family owns the little four-screen cinema in town, which means he gets to see free movies whenever he wants. And take whoever he wants. Panic swirls around in my stomach, making me feel like I might need to sit down. If Muffleman ends up dating Beth before I get the chance, it could ruin my life. I throw the ball back to Hai. It flies ten feet over his head, and he has to chase it.

"C'mon!" says Hai.

"Sorry. So what did he say?" I ask.

"Mate," Hai says, jogging back. "I don't know. He and some of his friends were talking about girls, and he mentioned that the new girl with glasses is pretty cute."

"And?"

Hai throws the ball right into my glove. "And," he says, "the other guys think so, too."

"Oh, no," I say, tossing my glove to the ground. "This is terrible."

"Well, what did you expect?" Hai says. "We live in pretty much the smallest town ever. Other boys are going to notice her."

"Ugh," I say, glancing over at the antique shop sitting over the road. "Why can't he like Liz or something?"

"Liz?" Hai laughs. "Really? People are afraid of Liz."

He's right. Even though the Markle girls are identical twins, they couldn't be more different. While Beth is quiet and sweet, Liz is loud and abrasive. Beth isn't exactly coordinated while Liz makes even the toughest guy in class nervous. Liz is a master at scowling while Beth's smile turns my heart into a gloppy mess.

"Muffleman," I say. "Why did it have to be Muffleman?"

"Well, if it isn't Muffleman," Hai says. "It'd just be some other boy." He's walking over, assuming I've finished tossing the ball. I've finished, all right.

"It's pretty sad," I say, knowing I sound like the most pathetic lad ever. "I'm actually hoping for another haunted antique just so I have an excuse to talk to her."

The problem with my plan is that a number of items that the Markles have sold from their antique shop have been haunted. And if people in town find out that their shop is selling haunted stuff, they'll stop shopping there. If they stop shopping there, they'll go out of business and move away.

Since I don't want that to happen, my best friend Hai and I have already helped them out a couple times. We figured out why a ghost was attached to an old hockey puck and why an antique record player didn't work any more. It's weird. None of us ever asked to become resident ghost experts or anything. Just like Beth didn't realize until she moved in that she can sometimes hear and feel when ghosts are around.

Just like I can't help falling for Beth.

Hai takes his glove off and tosses it high into the air. "Well," Hai says, catching the glove, "you've got to do something. Waiting around is pretty sad. Maybe you just need to tell her how you feel."

"That sounds like a terrible idea," I say. "I could never tell her I like her as more than a friend. I'd probably scare her away."

Hai shrugs.

I stare at him.

"What?" he says.

"Why should I listen to you, anyway?" I ask. "It's not like you've ever had a girlfriend."

"True," Hai says. "But neither have you."

I don't want to come off as some lovesick dummy. No one wants to hear any of that stuff, especially Hai, who's heard enough about Beth from me already. After hearing the horrible news about Muffleman, I decide I need to wash my sorrows down with something sugary. We head over to the Food Basket Convenience Store.

I find a bottle of Orange Twizt in the fridges in the back of the shop. Hai picks out a bottle of Rooty-Toot.

As we head to the till, a pile of cans crash to the ground, one aisle over.

"Clean up, aisle four," Hai says nice and loud, laughing.

A second later, we hear a familiar voice say, "Hai? Is that you? Is Casey with you?"

My heart feels like it just scored in the World Cup. I'm about to say something when I hear another voice.

"Seriously, Beth," the other voice says. "I swear you're the queen of clumsy."

This is it, I think to myself. My chance to knock Muffleman out of the picture!

We turn down the next aisle and see the Markle twins, Beth and Liz, in the middle of the row. There are cans of beans all over the floor.

"Crazy," Hai says, walking over to them. "How did you know it was us?"

I follow behind, trying to think of something, anything to say. I'm also hoping Hai doesn't mention our talk in the park.

"Our smart-aleck detector went wild," Liz says, standing over Beth, who is hurriedly trying to re-stack the cans. I get down on my knees to help her out. When I look up, we're just about face to face. As usual, I'm choking on words.

Beth smiles. "Hi, Casey," she says. "Thanks."

"Yeah," I say. "Hi. And sure. Yeah, okay. You're welcome."

"Well, this might just be fate," Liz says, shaking her head. "Beth was just talking about you."

I turn to Hai, thinking Liz is talking about him. When I look at Liz, I see she means me.

"Yes, you," Liz says.

"Oh," I say. "I was just talking about Beth, too, which is weird. Not that I think Beth is weird, of course. It's just that it's weird that we were both –"

"Go ahead and say something," Liz says to her twin, elbowing her.

"I don't know," Beth says. "I'm not sure how you'd feel about this, but I was hoping . . . "

I can feel Hai staring into the side of my head. I can feel Liz growing impatient with her sister. I can feel my shoulders tighten and my nerves freeze up.

"I was hoping that maybe you'd like to help us with a wagon we sold," Beth says.

My breath comes out in a rush after I realize that I'd been holding it. She's not asking me on a date or professing her love. But Beth Markle wants me to help her and her family figure out why something is haunted, again, and that's enough to make me ecstatic.

"Or maybe you're sick of the ghost stuff," Beth says when I don't respond right away.

"No, no," I say. "I could help you out. We make a great team. I mean, we all make a great team. Not just you and I, but you, Liz, Hai and me. We're like ghost hunters or something."

Beth raises her eyebrows a bit.

"Eh," Hai says. "More like ghost helpers. We haven't done any actual hunting."

"Ghost helpers?" Liz says as if trying the words out. "That sounds really lame."

As they argue about what our rag-tag team really should be called, I face Beth and manage a true, not-at-all-disappointed smile.

"We'll help you," I say. "Sure thing."

I didn't realize that "helping out" is what we'd be doing right away, but that's what's happening. We're walking to Jim Miller's house. He's a man that works at the small garage in town.

"So what's the deal?" I ask. "You guys sold another haunted antique?"

Beth nods. "I guess so," she says. "It was an old, rusty wagon from Red's collection of stuff. Liz looked up the listing in the diary."

"Yeah," Liz says. "It belonged to some old guy in town who's still alive."

"Really?" I ask. "You mean it's haunted, but the guy who owned it isn't dead?"

"I guess I'm not sure what's up," says Liz. "That's what we need to find out."

We turn into Cross Street and head down towards the end of the road. As we get to the Miller's house, I can see Jim and his wife, Sarah, standing on the front lawn. Their garage door is open. Inside are two sweet-looking classic cars.

"Oh, wow," Hai says in a whisper.

I'm so busy looking at the cars that it takes me a moment to notice the small wagon tied to the refurbished petrol pump at the edge of the driveway.

The wagon is moving back and forth on its own, straining against the rope.

The four of us stop in our tracks a house away from the Miller's, just watching.

"This ghost isn't shy about making itself known," Liz says. "Good grief, that's creepy."

Beth takes a couple cautious steps forward and seems like she's sensing something. The wagon rocks back and forth, pulling at the rope like a dog on a lead hoping to chase a squirrel.

"I'm not sure how we're going to explain this one," I say. There's no way these people won't assume the old wagon they bought isn't haunted. No way. I have a feeling that the Markles' reputation for selling creepy antiques is going to spread through Stonewick no matter what we do.

Even so, we follow Beth further down the pavement to the Miller's driveway.

"Mr Miller?" Beth asks, walking towards the couple. We follow along like her loyal followers, not sure what part we'll be able to play.

"Yes," Jim Miller says and walks over. "And you are?"

"I'm Beth Markle," Beth says. "My parents own Days Gone Buy. I hear you're having trouble with the wagon you bought."

Jim turns to Sarah, who raises her eyebrows. Both of them nod to the old wagon.

The wagon shifts back and forth along the driveway. I guess that's why they don't really need to say anything.

"It didn't do this back at the shop," Jim says, shaking his head. "But it's the darndest thing. I brought it home with plans to restore it, and it just started rolling down the driveway towards the street."

"Your driveway is nice and flat, which rules out gravity, I suppose," says Hai. "It's not like you're on a hill or anything."

"Right," Jim says. "Even so, I tied it to the petrol pump so it wouldn't roll away."

"That's when it started just going back and forth," Sarah says. "It's been doing this for some time."

Beth nods.

I can see in her expression that something else is going on. She's holding back.

"Do you mind if we take a look?" I ask.

Jim shrugs and motions to the wagon. "Help yourself," he says.

I walk over to the wagon and catch myself saying, "Take it easy, boy," like it's some sort of over-excited dog. I squat next to the old wagon to check it out. Barely any red paint remains on the body. It's so rusty, it looks like it's been left out in the rain for a few decades. The words Rockin' Roller appear on the body in a faded white script if you look closely enough.

I carefully place my hand on the rough edge of the wagon as if trying to calm it down. It's ice cold to the touch, even though it's sitting outside in the sun.

As if reacting to me, the antique begins to move back and forth even more quickly. I remove my hand.

"That's strange," I say.

"Yeah," Jim says. "That's putting it lightly. I already ordered the paint to re-do the body, but it's just bizarre. I'm afraid I'm just going to have to return it."

"We don't offer refunds," Liz says as if she's been preprogrammed to say that.

"But," I say quickly, "if you'd give us a little time to check it out, maybe we can figure out what's happening."

"I think it's possessed," Sarah says. "It seems like there's a poltergeist or something inside of that wagon."

"Don't say that," Jim says to Sarah.

Sarah folds her arms.

Jim looks at us. "We don't really believe in that stuff."

We do, I think to myself.

The rest of our group is silent, which doesn't help our cause too much. Someone's got to say something, so I say, "I'm sure there's an explanation. Like, some scientific explanation behind it."

"Maybe magnets," Hai says. "Earth's rotation or some stuff like that."

Both Jim and Sarah stare at us like we're crazy.

"Anyway," I say. "Can we take it for a while? Look into it, and let you know what we find?"

Jim looks at Sarah, who shrugs.

"That's fine," she says. "If that thing has a demon in it, though, I don't want it here."

"It's not a demon, honey," Jim says and shakes his head.

"I guarantee it's not a demon," I say and begin to untie the wagon.

"How do you know?" Sarah asks.

"Well," I say. "Why would a demon possess a wagon? It's probably science."

I've got the wagon untied and try not to look at either Jim or Sarah Miller. I grab the rusty handle and can feel the cold dig into my palm. I really don't think it's a demon, but there's definitely a ghost attached. I just don't understand whose ghost it could be.

Five minutes later, we're walking down Cross Street, away from the Miller house.

"So we're in a right pickle," Liz says. "This thing is probably more haunted than anything else we've sold."

"More haunted?" Hai says. "Really? Do you have a slide rule to measure how haunted something is?"

"Oh, shut up," Liz says.

Right now, we're all a bit confused as to what's happening. I notice that Beth is walking along as if in a trance. I want her to snap out of it and tell us what she's heard or seen.

As I pull the wagon along, I notice that the wagon's handle isn't cold any more. I tilt the handle back so it rests on the front of the wagon. It doesn't move.

"There," Liz says. "Case closed. The ghost has finished with it."

"He's not," Beth says in a whisper. "He just doesn't have the energy any more."

"He?" I say. "What are you feeling, Beth?"

Beth adjusts her glasses. "There was a lot of energy in this," Beth says, putting her hand on the wagon's handle. "But it's gone now. He was very excited to see us."

"You said 'he' again," I say.

"I know," Beth says. "I just don't know who he is yet. I'm just getting fragments."

"Either way," Hai says, "we sounded like idiots up there with no explanation as to what was wrong with this thing. I wanted to tell them that they were probably right, that the wagon is possessed."

"This is getting annoying," Liz says. "It's not our fault some of this old junk is haunted."

Beth sighs. "You shouldn't say that," she says quietly. "These items were all important to the spirits attached to them."

"Well, what do we do?" I ask. "Maybe talk to the guy in town who owned the wagon?"

"That'd be a weird conversation," Hai says. "'Hi, sir. We have this old wagon you used to own, but now it's haunted. Any idea why that might be?'"

Beth faces us and nods. "I think that's a great idea, Casey," she says.

Liz groans, which makes me wonder why she even bothers coming along with us in the first place. Maybe she feels some sense of duty since it's her parents' shop. Or, maybe she really wants to make sure no more refunds are issued.

"Well, what's the name of the guy who used to own it?" I ask and look at Liz. "Do you remember?"

"It's like Whistle or something," Liz says. "Bill Whistle, maybe."

"Seriously?" Hai asks, then laughs. "What kind of a name is that?"

"Wait," says Liz. "I remember now. It's Arnold Whittle. I was close."

"Bill Whistle was close?" Hai says. "That's hilarious."

Liz pinches her fingers together. "Did you know you're about this close to getting a kick in the trousers?" Liz says.

It takes me a minute, but I suddenly remember who Arnold Whittle is. Maybe it's because I've lived in Stonewick the longest.

"Arnold Whittle," I say. "His place is five minutes from here. Over in the Lone Oak block of flats."

No one seems excited to go, but this seems to be our best bet.

"What're we waiting for?" Hai asks. "Let's go and ask this Whittle guy about his haunted wagon."

The flats at Lone Oak really aren't much to write home about. They're the only flats in Stonewick. When we arrive, we're pulling the rusty wagon along with us.

We stand in front of the building. The place doesn't seem inviting at all. In the middle of the patchy lawn lies a sun-faded plastic tea set, face down in a muddy puddle. A pile of sodden newspapers deteriorate the front porch. Maybe whoever subscribed to the paper couldn't be bothered to come and get them.

"Wow," Liz says. "This place looks haunted, never mind the wagon."

We walk up the cracked pavement to the cluttered front porch. Along the inner wall is a panel with ten buttons on it. The names are faded and washed out a bit, but I scan the names until I see *A. WHITTLE*.

"Here goes," I say and press the button before any of us change our minds.

A weak-sounding whine squeaks out of the speaker until I release the button.

"Well, too bad," Hai says. "Nobody home." He's turning on his heel like he's planning to walk away.

A second later, a click precedes a gruff voice that says, "Yes?"

Hai stops dead in his tracks.

H. WHITE

I.J. SILVER

V. BARBOSA

Y. ISHIGAKI

C. MOLTISANTI

E. GUTHRIE

N. YOUNG

A. WHITTLE

H. BROOD

C.H. TURNER

I speak up. "Hi," I say. "Mr Whittle? My name is Casey Willis."

"Who?" says the voice. "Who is this?"

"I think we have your old wagon," I say quickly, thinking he's going to tell us to get lost. "I was hoping we could talk to you about it."

A long pause hangs in the air, and I glance at everyone else. Beth has her fingers woven together like she's saying a quick prayer.

The intercom speaker crackles a bit, and Mr Whittle speaks again. "I got rid of that wagon a long time ago," he says. "And I don't ever want to see it again."

Just when I think we've hit another dead end, I feel a chill. The air in the doorway of Lone Oak Flats feels charged, almost electric. Beth shudders and sighs.

"It's his brother," Beth whispers. A spooky look widens her eyes. "He wants to make it right." Her mouth is part way open as if she's still listening to things. It makes me shiver.

"Are you still there?" says Mr Whittle. "If so, please go away."

"Your brother," I blurt. "We think your brother is trying to reach you."

There's another long pause. I begin feeling bad for not only bugging this guy but bringing up his dead brother.

"I don't know what kind of sick joke you think you're playing," Mr Whittle says through the intercom. "But I don't appreciate it. I didn't want to talk to my brother before, and I certainly don't want to now. Goodbye."

A click lets us know he's done with us.

"That went well," Liz says.

◆

We walk back from the flat, heading towards my street. Beth still appears as if she's been startled by something from the beyond, and the rest of us are quiet, puzzled.

"So who's his brother?" I say.

"Peter," Beth says. "Mr. Whittle's brother's name is Peter."

Liz shudders. "You are so creepy, Beth," she says. "Seriously. I don't think I can ever get used to this."

"I can't help it, "Beth says. She fixes her glasses and blows a strand of hair out of her face.

"So," I say, "we know that Peter is trying to reach Arnold somehow, right?"

"I guess," Beth says.

"Why?" I ask.

"He's not saying much else," says Beth. "It's like he's exhausted."

"Probably from all the wagon action over at the Miller house," Hai says. "It takes a lot of energy for ghosts to move stuff, doesn't it?"

I look at Hai like he just grew a second nose on his face. Liz does, too.

"What?" he says. "Maybe I've researched some ghost stuff online lately. Big deal."

"Okay," I say. "So maybe we go to the library and look up what we can about Peter Whittle. Maybe we'll discover something new."

"It's almost five," Liz says. "Doesn't the library close early at the weekends?"

The darkening sky proves it's getting late.

"Mrs Gulliver has probably locked up for the night," I say. "Maybe tomorrow? We've had luck at the library before. Maybe we will again."

"Sure," Hai says. "So who's taking the wagon home?"

No one offers.

"Why don't you?" I ask, looking at Hai.

"Are you kidding?" Hai says. "If that rusty monster starts moving around, my little sisters will freak."

Liz folds her arms and addresses Beth.

"I don't think we should, either," Liz says. "We bring it back to the store, and Mum and Dad will wonder why we keep bringing home the stuff we've sold."

"Perfect," I say. "I guess that leaves me."

After I say it, Beth smiles at me like I'm doing the bravest, nicest deed possible.

"I'll do it," I say. "Hopefully, old Peter is worn out from his active afternoon."

I pull the old Rockin' Roller up the pavement and to the wooden steps that lead to our front porch. I stop and look at the wagon. I even listen to it. Unlike Beth, who can actually hear the voices of the dead, I hear absolutely nothing.

"What's with the old wagon?" my dad asks.

The wagon is silent.

"Just helping out the Markle twins," I say. "A customer thought something was wrong with it, so we're going to try and fix it tomorrow."

"I think that old rust bucket is beyond fixing," Dad says, sifting through the post.

I tug it up the stairs and roll it into the veranda. I figure this is the best place for it. Out of my personal sight for the night. Somewhere I don't have to think about it. I toss my baseball glove in there, too.

"You've been spending some time with those Markle girls," Dad said. "You and Hai like those two?"

"What do you mean?" I say quickly.

Dad puts his hands up like I just pulled a pistol out of a gun belt.

"Easy," Dad says. "Just asking."

"Sorry," I say, expelling some air out of my lungs. "They're okay. Liz is kind of crabby a lot."

"Well, what about the other one?"

"Beth?" I say, beginning to fidget.

"Wait a second," Dad says. "They're twins and their names are Beth and Liz?"

"Beth is short for Bethany," I say. "Liz is short for Lizette. They're not alike, though."

Dad shakes his head and raises his eyebrows and doesn't say anything else for a moment. I'm ready to go inside.

"Well if you like this Beth gal, you might be in luck," he says.

"What?" I ask and pause. "What do you mean?"

Dad unfolds a piece of paper he's got in his hands. It's the spring term school newsletter. He hands the paper to me and smiles.

"Looks like they're doing a fund-raiser this coming Friday," he says.

I don't get where he's going at all, so I take a look at the newsletter for myself. Dad points to a passage.

"Spring Fever Disco?" I read. "Yeah, I don't really do discos."

"That's because you've never been to one," Dad says, cuffing my ear. "Maybe you could work on some moves, show this lady who owns the dance floor."

Yeah right, I think sarcastically. *That sounds exactly like me.*

My mum calls from inside, and my dad goes into the house, leaving me with the newsletter. I read the few details provided. Years seven to nine are invited. A fiver to get in.

"Forget it," I say out loud. I watch the sun slip lower in the sky. I'd invite Beth . . . if I could talk to her about something other than dead people haunting stuff. Which reminds me, I have a haunted wagon on my veranda, and it's going to be dark soon.

Later in the evening I sit in the living room, playing my semi-new video game, *Digi-Tanks 2: The Wreck-oning*. I've improved, but so has Hai. If I want to able to compete with him, I need to put in some serious controller time on my own. My parents are watching some show in their room since I've commandeered the big TV for my video games. As I'm roving the digital wasteland, looking for another camp of toxic bandits to assault, I hear a dull thud just outside our front door.

THUMP.

I press the pause button, halting the onscreen action so I can listen.

THUMP. THUMP.

I know what it is, but I don't want it to be what I think it is. I set my controller down, stand up and go to the front door. I part the white curtains over the door's window and take a look out onto the veranda. It's dark, so I don't see a thing.

Please wait until tomorrow, I think.

I reach over to switch on the veranda lights. The light illuminates a couple of wicker chairs, my baseball glove, Mum's neglected plants and the wagon. It's not moving. I turn my head and wonder where the noise came from. I eyeball the veranda door, thinking maybe the wind is to blame, but it's latched tight.

My heart hammers in my chest. As I turn and look at the wagon again, it moves, just slightly. Its front end thumps into the side of the veranda. It's like watching a remote control car that's running low on batteries driving weakly into a wall.

THUMP. THUMP.

I watch to see if the wagon does it again. Both Hai and Beth said it's possible the ghost is exhausted. As I step away from the window, I realize I'm pretty tired, too. After the wagon stays still for a minute or so, I try to relax.

I switch off my video games, turn off the TV and get ready for bed. My parents are still watching their movie, so I pop in to say good night before heading to my room. I turn off all of the lights in my bedroom. Well, all but my desk lamp.

I hop into bed and try to sleep. I listen for any noises but don't hear any. I start to think about Peter Whittle and why he might be haunting a wagon.

Who haunts a wagon? I think. I realize it's just as strange as a haunted hockey puck or a ghostly record player, but still. Why haunt something that doesn't belong to you? There has to be a reason.

I flip over on my side and see that the corner of my room is really dark, over near my dresser. What if Peter is standing there watching me right now? Who says the ghost has to stay with the wagon? Did I just haunt my own house? Why did I agree to bring the wagon home?

I close my eyes. It would be nice to fast-forward the night. Morning seems safer.

I think about Peter. We don't know anything about him. Maybe he was a bad guy. Maybe that's why his brother Arnold doesn't want to hear from him. What if Peter was evil? What if we are getting in way over our heads? Why didn't I have Hai to stay over tonight?

THUMP. THUMP. THUMP. THUMP.

It's faint, but it's enough to sit me straight up in my bed. My ears ring with fear like they sometimes do when I wake up from a nightmare. It's chilly in my room, but my skin feels warm enough to set my clothes on fire.

I get out of bed, not quite sure what to do. I open my bedroom door and peer down the hallway. The light is out in my parents' room, and I don't see the flickering light from the TV in there, either. They're asleep . . . at least for now.

Telling myself I'm crazy, I slip out into the hallway and head downstairs. I flip on the light in the kitchen and then walk into the living room. Crouching low, I slink over to the window that looks onto the front veranda. I peek through the mini-blinds. What I see nearly makes me lose all the strength in my legs.

A shadowy figure has materialized on my veranda. It's faded and dark, but I make out a distinct head, arms, and hands. The apparition is gripping the base of the wagon and pulling it. With each attempt, the front of the wagon bangs against the wall. It's as if Peter is trying to pull the rusty thing through the veranda.

But the craziest part? I can see him.

I don't know what to do. Part of me wants to call Hai or the Markles to see if anyone can help me.

Another part of me wants to run up into my parents' room, throw on the lights, and cry.

Instead, I do something else.

I walk over to the front door, and before I can talk myself out of it, I open it. I step onto the front veranda. It's cold, like stepping onto a frozen lake with bare feet.

"Hey," I whisper. "Peter."

I can still see the shadowy figure grabbing at the wagon. It's taking all of my energy not to scream.

"We're going to help you," I say, feeling my voice shudder with fear. I almost expect flowerpots and my dad's old lawn-mowing shoes to fly at me.

THUMP. THUMP. THUMP.

He's still pulling at the wagon.

"Please stop," I say. "We can't do anything until tomorrow."

And just like that, the wagon stops moving and the shadowy figure disappears.

The library doesn't open until early
afternoon, but I'm here waiting in front of the
place for everyone else to show up. I wasn't too
excited to drag the wagon across town to the
Stonewick Library, but I did it.

With an old bike chain and lock I found in
the garage, I thread one end through the wagon
handle, around the wheel axles and lock it
up. I spin the combination to 000. It probably
seems pretty ridiculous, locking up an old,
rusty wagon. But I have a feeling that this thing
would take off if it could.

A small two-door car pulls into the car park. The driver kills the engine and opens a door squeaky enough to give all of the dogs in town a headache. "Well, this is what I like to see," Mrs Gulliver says. "A young reader just waiting for the library to open!"

I wave to the old librarian. She's got her handbag and a stack of books in her arms. She kicks her car door closed and walks over, fumbling for the keys.

"Hi, Mrs Gulliver," I say. "Need a hand?"

I help her with the books as she fits the key in the lock and opens up our town's ancient library. It's dark inside, but I can't say it's quiet. Faint music hums in the background, and it sends a quick chill along the hairs on my arms.

"Good afternoon, Claudette," Mrs Gulliver calls out.

The music I hear is an old song, but one I've become familiar with since our last ghostly adventure. It's the song "Moonlight Romance" by a guy named Billy Sommers. When I peer through the dim library, I can see the old phonograph playing from the main desk towards the front.

"She still plays that song all the time?" I ask, setting the books on the counter.

"At least when the library is closed she does," Mrs Gulliver says with a smile. "But she knows that once we're open, the library needs to be quiet. Right, Claudette?"

And just like that, the needle arm of the old phonograph rises up. It returns to the cradle, and the turntable stops spinning. I know the ghost of Claudette Barnes would never do any harm to anyone, but it's still really eerie to see.

The front door opens behind us. Hai and the Markle twins have arrived.

"So much business right away," Mrs Gulliver says. "Let me just get the lights."

Before Mrs Gulliver can head towards the bank of switches, they all click on, casting a little more light on the dim library.

"Okay," Liz says, looking up at the lights. "I'm ready to leave now."

"Don't be silly," Mrs Gulliver says, waving her off. "Claudette's just being helpful."

As the librarian gets the library up and running, the four of us head to a table near the old, stained glass windows.

"She's really happy here," Beth says, smiling.

"No, I'm not," Liz says. "This library is creepier than ever."

"I mean Claudette," Beth says. "I can feel that she's at peace."

I peer around, wondering if Claudette's ghost is watching or listening to us. Maybe she's even seen Peter's ghost hovering around near the wagon. I'm not sure. I don't know how stuff like that works in the ghost world.

"How did last night go, Casey?" Hai says.

"Terrible," I say. "The wagon started moving around last night. I thought he might wake up my parents. I went downstairs and . . . " I trail off, thinking about the shadow figure reaching through the walls of our front veranda.

"What happened, Casey?" Beth's eyes are wide with worry.

"I saw him," I say. "Like his shadow or something. I told him we wanted to help him and that we needed to wait until today to do it. So he stopped."

"Fantastic," Liz says. "But what if we can't help him?"

"Full refund, I guess," I say and shrug.

Since the computer in our library is an old, antique piece of junk that can't even access the internet, searching for info about the Whittle brothers is extra tricky.

Hai is able to find a link on his phone from the *Stonewick Gazette* that mentions something about Peter Whittle, but when he clicks on it, an error message appears. "All I've got is a date," Hai says. "But it doesn't give me any more information."

"Weird," I say. "I've never heard of the *Stonewick Gazette*."

"That's because they haven't printed a newspaper in close to twenty years," Mrs Gulliver says as she shelves a few books nearby.

"I don't suppose you've got a pile of these old *Gazettes* lying around," Liz says, folding her arms.

"Even better," Mrs Gulliver says.

We follow her to some weird machine sitting on a table in the corner. The device is fitted with a small screen and what looks like a flat, square plate with a little handle attached to it. To the left, a disorganized heap of folders sits in a pile.

The machine looks like something out of an old science fiction movie.

"What is this?" I ask.

"It's our microfiche machine," Mrs Gulliver says almost proudly. "It hasn't been used as much in recent days, so we've actually thought of throwing it out, sad to say."

"I'm not even sure anyone knows what this thing is," Liz says.

Mrs Gulliver runs her hands along the top of the giant screen as if dusting it with her thin fingers.

"Back before the internet, important information was archived using microfiche," Mrs Gulliver says. "It's a tiny picture of a document that can be magnified so that you can read it."

I step closer. Inside the folders are plastic sheets. I pull one out and hold it to the light.

"These are documents?" I ask. "They're so tiny." Really, all I can see are a load of nearly microscopic squares.

"They're tiny until you use the viewer," Mrs Gulliver says. She grabs the lead and disappears under the table to plug it in.

"I'm not sure how this will help us," Hai says. "We need to find an article from the *Stonewick Gazette*."

The machine hums to life, and the light beneath the monitor blips on. A moment later, Mrs Gulliver climbs out from under the desk.

"As it happens, we've got every article ever published in the *Gazette* here," Mrs Gulliver says, standing up. She sifts through the folders and pulls one out that's labelled "SG" in her shaky handwriting"

The thick folder is completely crammed full of old films.

Liz groans. "This is going to take forever," she says.

It doesn't take forever. Hai pulls up the dead link he found on his phone, which has a date attached to it. We open up the folder and find a number of films within the same time period.

Thankfully, the *Stonewick Gazette* was a weekly paper, not a daily. After a little digging, Beth finds something.

"Here, Casey," she says, handing it to me. "Let's find out what happened to Peter Whittle."

We tell Mrs Gulliver enough to satisfy her curiosity. She helps me load the microfiche, and soon I'm zipping around through the articles. I skip news about businesses opening, countless crop reports and a story about a lost cow that was never found.

"All boring small town stuff," Liz says, reading over my shoulder. "No wonder the paper closed down."

I slide to the next page. I find a small blurb with an old picture near it. In seconds, I know I have found the article.

The picture shows a crowd of men in hats and old, farmer-looking clothes standing on the edge of a river. They don't look like they're there for fun. A stern-looking man holds up a wagon.

"That's the wagon," Hai whispers and points. "The Rollin' Rocker."

I zoom in on the text and read the short article a reporter named Stephen Crawford wrote.

"The community was devastated when they discovered the body of thirteen-year-old local boy, Peter Whittle, on Tuesday," I say, reading aloud. *"Friends and neighbours had learned that Peter had fallen into the river a few days earlier. Local volunteers searched for him for days. His younger brother, eight-year-old Arnold Whittle, indicated that Peter had been racing down the nearby hill at the south end of the Dyer farmland in a small wagon before crashing and landing in the river."*

"Oh no," Beth says, making me stop. "He used his brother's wagon to –"

"Do something stupid," Liz says. "How are we supposed to do anything about that?"

"*Peter Whittle's body was discovered downstream by a search team of local men, led by shop-owner Bill Redcliffe,*" I read, continuing the short article. "*Medical personnel believe that Whittle's head struck a rock, killing the boy instantly.*"

"And Arnold saw the whole thing," Beth whispers. "This is horrible."

For a minute, the hum of the machine is the only sound.

"So why would Arnold not want to talk to his brother?" Beth asks quietly.

"Maybe because he's dead," Liz says.

I cringe. "That doesn't seem right," I say. "In our brief talk with Arnold Whittle through the intercom, he said he didn't want to talk to him before, and he doesn't want to now."

Beth pushes her glasses up. "He was mad at Peter even before he died," she says.

"But why?" I ask, wishing they'd written a newspaper article about that.

◆

We're standing outside the library near the chained-up wagon.

Hai points at it and raises his eyebrows. "Were you thinking someone was going to steal it or something?" Hai asks.

"No, genius," I say. "I didn't want the wagon to wander off. How would I explain that? 'Oh hi, Mr Miller. Yeah, we were going to fix your wagon, but it got away from us. Sorry about that.'"

Both Liz and Beth laugh.

I crouch down to unlock the lock.

"I just can't imagine what happened," Beth says. "What made Arnold so mad that even after his brother's death he's still –"

Before she can finish, the wagon, free from its chain, is off like a shot.

"No way!" says Hai.

The wagon rumbles down the path in front of the library and jumps over the curb. Rust snowflakes from the bottom of the wagon as it rattles across the car park.

"Let's go after it!" says Hai.

We all sprint after the runaway wagon. Looking, surely, like fools.

"Where's it going?" I ask as the wagon turns on its own down Maple Street.

"Why don't you ask it?" Liz says, flying past.

She runs much faster than any of us and steadily gains on the wagon. When she's almost reached it, she reaches out to grab it.

Beth shouts, "No Liz! Let it go!"

"Are you serious?" Liz shouts over her shoulder.

When I see the wagon make another turn, I realize it's not going to Arnold's home. "She's right!" I shout. "Let it go! We just need to follow its lead."

Liz drops back, and we jog behind the wagon. It goes for a few more minutes to the wooded area lining the eastern edge of town. When the pavement ends, it rumbles across the wet, soggy ground.

"Mud on the tyres," Liz says. "That wagon is going to be a mess when we get it back."

"The Millers don't want it if it's haunted," I say. "Mud or no mud."

As the wagon rolls through the longer grass and through some bushes, I begin to wonder, *Is this thing taking us to the river?*

It's been a long winter of no running around and spending a lot of time indoors, so I'll admit that I'm feeling winded after our five minute run. I'm relieved when it finally comes to a stop beneath a large, moss-covered tree.

"Whoa," says Hai, looking up. "There's an old tree house up there."

Calling what we found a tree house is being really generous. It's more like a rotting wooden shack up in a giant, old tree. Even so, none of us have ever seen it before.

"Is this where he wanted to take us?" I ask, not expecting an answer.

"Yes," Beth says. She's got her hand on the wagon.

"I thought maybe he was heading back to the river," Hai says.

Both Liz and I tilt our heads until we are looking up at the tree house. A fragile-looking rope ladder hangs from the tree and leads up to the tree house.

"It's too high to reach," I say.

"Not if you step on the wagon," Liz says.

"I don't want to climb up there," I say.

"I don't want to either," Liz says. "This place gives me the creeps. In a big way."

Hai is shaking his head at me. I almost want to complain that I took one for the team last night by keeping the wagon at my house, but I don't. Beth is watching me like she expects me to say something.

"Okay," I say. "Let's see if I can even reach."

I take a careful step on the wagon, afraid that Peter may take off again, and I'll fall on my face. The wagon stays put as I reach up high. My fingers can barely reach the bottom rung.

"It's too high," I say. As soon as I say that, I feel the air around me change. It's like the wind stops and everything around me freezes. A cool sensation envelops my legs, and I feel myself boosted. I grasp the bottom rung and pull myself up.

"Casey, are you okay?" Beth calls. It's like she can sense what just happened.

"I just got a boost," I whisper, like I'm afraid I'm going to wake up the rest of the woods.

I climb to the next rung. It's wet and soggy. Thankfully, none of the pieces come loose.

Once I make it the rest of the way up and in, I call down to the others that I have made it.

An old piece of sodden carpeting covers the platform. A chair made of more rust than metal lies on its side. Boards are missing here and there on the floor and on the sides, and the boards that exist are rotting away. The back wall is completely gone, giving me a great view of the woods. It's not the safest tree house ever.

I'm surprised to hear Beth and the others climbing up, too.

"Not much here," Hai says, reaching the top.

"Nope," I say. It's pretty hard not to be disappointed. "Not much at all."

Beth comes next. I grab hold of her hand to help her up, and it's awesome. Even if it's only for a second.

"Thanks, Casey," Beth says. Before I've fully enjoyed the moment, she says, "Oh. Peter's up here with us."

As Liz climbs up, I can see she's not impressed. "We chased after the wagon for this?" she says.

Beth puts her hand on the floor and closes her eyes like she's feeling or hearing something we can't. "He's saying, 'I'm sorry, Arnie. I'm so sorry,'" Beth whispers. "He's saying it over and over again."

"Is he saying anything else?" I ask.

"No," Beth says. "He's weak now."

"Well, yeah," Liz says. "He just led us across town on a wild goose chase."

"Probably just wanted us to see this sweet tree house," Hai said. "Pretty cool, man."

Peter's finished talking to us, so we begin to climb back down, one-by-one. I'm the last one to go. When I put my foot on the top rung, the air grows cool around me, and I hear a slight metallic rattling noise. I stop what I'm doing.

"Let's go, Willis," Hai shouts from the ground below. "Are you coming down or what?"

"Hold on," I say. "Be quiet for a sec."

I listen again, and there it is. I climb back up and stand in the tree house. I hear the metal clacking again as a slight breeze blows across the tops of the trees. I turn. Something moves on the moss-covered back of the giant tree that the tree house is built around.

It's a key.

A rusty nail has been driven through the top

of the key, pinning it into the tree itself. The key is tinged with rust and blue corrosion. It's probably been there a long, long time.

"I've found something," I say.

"What is it?" says Hai.

I reach out and touch it. It's gritty against my fingertips. I try to grasp the key to pull it free, but it's staying put.

I re-adjust my grasp on the key and pull. I feel the nail loosening. When I give it another tug, the key comes free from the bark, but I stumble backwards. I'm about to fall from out of the back of the tree house.

I wave my arms to regain my balance. It's a long way down, and I'm going to end up as dead as Peter Whittle.

Just before I fall, I cry out.

A cold, invisible hand grabs me right in the middle of my sweatshirt and secures me, saving me from falling. My chest tightens against the instant chill.

I fall to my knees in the middle of the tree house, and the key clatters down on the warped wood next to me. "Thanks," I say, panting.

The ghost of Peter Whittle just saved my life.

9

"What happened to you up there?" Hai asks.

"I almost fell," I say and hold up the key. "I was trying to pull this out of the tree."

The rest of the group gathers around to look. I think about telling them that Peter's ghost helped me, but I don't.

Beth takes the key from my hand and closes her eyes tightly. "This is what we came here for," Beth says. "This is what Peter wanted us to find."

"Perfect," Liz says. "Let's take the key to his brother and see if that does it."

Suddenly, the wagon begins to move again. It heads deeper into the woods.

"Hey!" Liz says, calling to the wagon. "Your brother lives back this way!"

"I don't think that's it," I say.

"Of course not," Liz mumbles.

We follow the wagon through the woods. I'd never really thought to explore this place before, but it's actually really pretty cool. The trees are gigantic, and the weathered trunks are thick with branches and large wooded, bark-covered lumps.

"Those trees look like they've got boils," Hai says. "Or tumours or something."

After a bit of a walk, we find ourselves in an empty field. A cluster of pine trees stand up like arrows, pointing into the blue sky. The wagon comes to a creaky halt in the middle of the damp grass.

"Is he worn out?" I ask. I turn around once but don't see anything like the tree house for us to explore.

"No," Beth says. "He wants us to dig."

"Whoa, whoa," Hai says. "No way. We're not going to dig up his body."

"What?" I say. "Why do you think there's a body here?"

Hai shrugs. "What if there is?" he says. "What if Peter Whittle is buried right here?"

Liz backs away from the wagon. Beth still holds the key, listening.

"We don't have a shovel," I say. "How are we supposed to dig?"

"I'll run and get one," Liz says, clearly looking for an excuse to leave us alone with the old, haunted wagon. "But if I do, someone else is doing the digging."

"I'm not doing it," Hai says. "Not a chance."

"I don't want to do it either," I say. "Who knows what's under there?"

"That's what I'm saying!" says Hai.

"You guys figure it out," Liz says. "Make a decision before I'm back."

And just like that, she's running through the woods like a deer fleeing from hunters.

"Beth," I say. "Do you have any idea what's under the ground here?"

Beth looks up like she was just roused from an afternoon nap. She shakes her head slowly but stares down at the ground as if there's a clue there.

"There's no reason there'd be a body beneath us," I say. "They found Peter Whittle's body in the river. Why would they just bury him out in the middle of the woods?"

"It's settled then," Hai says. "Since you know there's no body below us, you can do the digging."

"I'll do it," Beth says quietly. "If you guys don't want to."

And suddenly, I feel like a complete idiot for even arguing about digging. There's no way I'm going to just stand here and watch Beth Markle do the dirty – and scary – work.

"No, no," I say. "I can do it. Hai will fill the hole back up when we're done."

"Hey!" Hai shouts.

Just like I thought, Liz is back in no time at all with an old-looking shovel in her hand. She doesn't seem winded at all.

"Where'd you get that shovel?" Hai asks. I think he's thinking what I'm thinking.

"At the shop," Liz asks. "Why?"

"It wasn't from Red's collection of haunted junk in your cellar, was it?" says Hai.

"No," Liz says and tosses it down. "It was in with my dad's tools and stuff. Get digging."

Hai turns to me and smiles. I give him a dirty look and pick up the shovel.

The shovel is big and heavy. The last time I used a shovel, I was six. I tried to dig to earth's magma core but ended up stopping after about ten minutes and ten centimetres of work.

"Here goes nothing," I say.

Beth smiles at me, but I can see that it's fake. Something is bothering her. It's probably Peter Whittle's ghost, saying stuff.

I break through the first snarls of long grass. After that, thankfully, the ground is marshy and fairly easy to dig into. I position the blade into the dirt and jump onto the shovel's edges like it's a pogo stick. The shovel sinks into the earth, and I scoop another chunk out.

"I wonder how far down I have to dig," I say.

"If you see a human hand," Hai says, "go ahead and stop digging."

"Nice," I say. I keep at it.

After ten minutes, I've dug a pretty decent hole. Better than the one I made when I was six. So far, though, we haven't found anything. I start to wonder how good Peter's ghostly memory is. Or maybe he's playing a prank on us from the afterlife.

"He's excited," Beth says. "His energy feels positive and a bit wild."

"Sure," I say. "He's probably laughing at us. Chasing a wagon to dig a hole in the middle of the woods. Good old Sneaky Pete."

THUNK.

My shovel hits something solid. I freeze and stare at the ground.

"What is it, Willis?" Hai asks. "Did you hit bone?"

I pull the shovel blade out and drive it down again.

THUNK.

I toss the shovel aside and squat down near the hole, scooping and clawing at loose earth. Something is down there. When I touch it, I sense the feeling of cold metal. *It's a casket!* I think. *Hai was right all along!*

I pull more dirt out of the hole. I find an edge, and then a flat surface. There's a small handle on top of there.

"It's a metal box," I say.

I get my dirty fingers under the handle and pull. I can feel the box loosen within its earthy cradle a bit. I pull again and it comes free.

"This is it," Beth whispers. "We've found it."

I brush dirt and grime away. About the size of a kid's shoe box, it's rusty and definitely old. The words *NELSON STEELWORKS MANUFACTURING* is stamped on the side. I brush more grime from the box to reveal a raised, circular notch just below the lid.

"There's a lock," I say.

"We have the key," Beth says and hands it to me.

I rub the key between my thumb and fingers a few times as I look at the box. I can't even imagine what's inside. I guess I'm just relieved that it can't possibly be a dead body.

"Open it," Liz says. "What're you waiting for?"

Beth nods at me as if to tell me that Peter says it's all right to go ahead.

Using the end of the key, I scrape out some of the dirt in the keyhole. It's gritty and sends a shiver through my shoulders. When I fit the key to the lock, it sinks in cleanly. With a quick twist, I unlock the box and open the rusty lid.

"You have to be kidding me," Hai says, glancing over my shoulder. "Is that what I think it is?"

I peek into the box and see a baseball card covered in plastic. The smiling face of a baseball player looks back at us. A baseball bat is slung over his shoulder, and a stadium looms in the background.

"That card looks really, really old," I say. "Ancient, almost."

"David Williams," Liz says. "Pitcher for the Kodiaks."

I pick up the card and see that it's the only thing inside the box. It's in perfect condition, preserved for however long it was underground. I can't tell how old it is since I've never heard of David Williams or the Kodiaks, but someone thought it was worth protecting.

"So," I say, "why would Peter want us to find this old baseball card?"

"Dude," Hai says, his eyes wide. "You won't believe this." He holds up his phone.

I've seen ghosts. I've just chased a wagon through our town to dig up a buried baseball card. I'm one hundred per cent sure I'll believe whatever Hai's discovered.

Hai shows me his phone's screen. "This card is extremely rare. In mint condition, it's worth at least two hundred thousand dollars."

I don't believe it.

"We're rich," Hai shouts. "Holy crow, we could build our own baseball stadium!"

"Hold up," I say. "This doesn't belong to us."

Beth nods. "It's Arnold's card."

Liz groans. "Of course it is."

I hand the card to Beth and Hai and fill the hole back up with dirt. We need to make another visit to Lone Oak Flats.

I push the button marked A. WHITTLE on the flat's intercom.

When it takes longer than a second for anyone to answer, Hai is back at it. "See?" he says. "Not home. Guess we get to keep the card."

"Yes?" It's Arnold Whittle's voice on the intercom.

"Hi, Mr Whittle," I say. "My name is Casey Willis. We stopped by yesterday to tell you about your brother."

"I told you," he says, "to go away." The intercom's little speaker rattles from the volume of his voice.

"We have your David Williams baseball card," I say, interrupting him.

There's a long pause before he says, "I'll be right down."

A few minutes later, an old guy in a large green bathrobe opens the door and steps out into the front porch. Arnold Whittle wears horn-rimmed glasses with dirty lenses, has messy, white hair that's balding at the back and sports a patchy beard that could do with some cleaning up.

"What's this you said about my baseball card?" he says.

I hand over the buried treasure.

"I . . . I don't know what to say," Mr Whittle says. "How?"

Beth points to the wagon parked on the pavement. Ever since it led us to the dig site, it hasn't moved on its own. Even so, I'm guessing that Peter is present.

"That was my wagon," Mr Whittle says. "And it's what Peter rode when he . . . "

"We read about it," I say. "But we think Peter wanted you to have his card."

"It was mine from the start," Mr Whittle whispers. "It wasn't easy being his younger brother. Peter was always picking on me. Taking my belongings, excluding me from playing with his friends. He even built a tree house that I couldn't reach."

"Wow," Liz says in a quiet voice. "Not cool."

"This was the card I'd always wanted," Mr Whittle says. "And when I got this one, Peter took it and hid it from me."

"I've never heard of that guy," I say. "Was he any good?"

"David Williams grew up here in Stonewick," Mr Whittle says. "So when he made it to the big leagues, people around here were pretty excited, as you can imagine."

"Wow," Hai says. "And your brother never told you where it was?"

Mr Whittle looks at the card and shakes his head. His eyes water behind his glasses.

"He never had the chance," Mr Whittle says. "A week later he and his friends were racing in my wagon down Dyer Hill towards the river. That was the last time I saw him alive."

"I'm sorry," I say. "That must've been awful."

"It was," Mr Whittle says, drawing in a deep breath and letting out a loud sigh. "I was always angry with him, and when he died, I was even angrier. How could he do that? How could he leave me, doing something so stupid?"

We're all quiet for a moment. I'm not quite sure what to say.

"Peter says he's sorry," Beth says. "He's sorry for everything."

"Well . . . I forgive him," Mr Whittle says, wiping his eyes. "And I miss him. Every day."

I hear Beth exhale lightly, and by her facial expression, I know Peter has left her alone.

"I don't know how or where you kids found this," Mr Whittle says. "And maybe I don't want to know. But thank you."

We tell Mr Whittle we're glad we could help him. We wish him well.

As we're turning to leave, Hai spins back around to face Arnold Whittle. "What're you going to do with that card?" he asks. "That thing is worth a whole load of money, you know."

Mr Whittle holds the card up and smiles at it before looking back at Hai.

"I'm keeping it," Mr Whittle says. "It's worth a lot more than money to me."

After Hai heads to work at the restaurant and Liz returns to Days Gone Buy to put away the shovel, Beth and I walk the old wagon back to the Miller house. I feel good about everything we did today, but just like before, I have this feeling I won't talk to Beth again until we run into another ghost problem.

"So do you think Peter is better after all of this?" I ask.

"He's at peace finally," Beth says. "And he's moved on."

"That's a relief," I say.

"Thanks for helping me again, Casey."

"Oh," I say. "No problem. I like you."

My heart freezes like an ice cube. I think I meant to say, *I like to help you guys*, but that's not what came out.

"I like you, too, Casey," Beth says.

"I'm sorry, I didn't mean to . . . " I say, as if I hadn't just heard what she said. "Wait, what?"

"I like you," Beth says. "You're a great guy and a good friend."

"Wow," I say. My heart's beating so fast I'm finding it hard to make words come out.

"I just get a little shy sometimes," Beth says.

"Me too," I say. I keep looking down at the pavement, almost afraid to face Beth. "I never know what to say to girls."

Beth stops walking. I stop, too.

Before I know what's happening, she's giving me a hug. I hug her back.

"Sometimes you don't have to say a thing," she says, still holding on.

I'm smiling so hard I think my face is going to break. We let each other go, but I can't get the stupid grin off my face.

Beth laughs and shakes her head. "Let's get this wagon back to the Millers, okay?"

"Yeah," I say. "Okay. Let's do that. Wait. Do you think they'll even want it back? I mean, this rust bucket is what killed Peter Whittle."

"I don't know," Beth says. "But really, being reckless is why Peter died at a young age. It's just sad he used his brother's wagon for his stunt. But we can tell the Millers that, and let them decide."

"Sounds fair," I say and hope they'll take it anyway. I'd hate for the Markles to lose more business because the stuff in their cellar is haunted.

I want to ask Beth if she'll go with me to the Spring Fever Disco coming up. Maybe she'll want to see a movie at Muffleman's cinema.

But for now, I'm just enjoying the moment. I'll have time later to ask her all that stuff.

Maybe tomorrow.

CRY BABY HOLLOW

The first children's wagons were designed to be a smaller versions of horse-drawn wagons. In the 1800s, a family rode a horse-drawn wagon across a bridge in Hartselle, Alabama, USA. One of the wheels snapped and the wagon overturned, ejecting an infant into the river. Sadly, the baby drowned in the accident. Today, some believe that if you go to the bridge at night, you can hear the sounds of a baby crying and its mother sobbing. The area is now known locally as Cry Baby Hollow.

ABOUT THE AUTHOR

Thomas Kingsley Troupe was afraid of just about everything as a kid. Now a full-fledged adult, he's become fascinated by the creepy, the strange, and the unexplained. In his spare time, he investigates ghostly activity with the Twin Cities Paranormal Society. With his own ghost squad, he's stayed in a few haunted places, including the Stanley Hotel in Colorado, USA, and the Villisca Murder House in Iowa, USA.

ABOUT THE ILLUSTRATOR

Rudy-Jan Faber lives and works in the beautiful town of Leeuwarden in the Netherlands. Whenever Rudy has some time to spare, he loves to lock himself up in his attic and paint with oils. After leaving his job as a concept artist at a gaming studio, Rudy took up his passion for book illustration. He loves it when he can make illustrations for super spooky stories . . . or for stories with pirates or for super spooky stories with pirates.

GLOSSARY

apparition ghost or spirit of a dead person

bizarre very strange or odd

clumsy careless and awkward in the way that one moves or behaves

corrosion destroyed or eaten away at until it has disappeared little by little

deteriorate to get worse

fidget to keep moving because one is bored, nervous or uneasy

fragment small piece or part that is broken off

metallic hard, shiny or having a make-up of metal

microfiche flat piece of film containing microphotographs of pages of a newspaper or other document

poltergeist ghost that makes strange noises and causes objects to move

FURTHER INVESTIGATION

1. Casey ends up taking the wagon to his house and is stuck digging the spot up in the woods. Why did he volunteer to do something he didn't really want to do?

2. Arnold Whittle didn't get along with his older brother Peter and held a grudge, even after Peter died. Why? Do you know of anyone who has held a grudge?

3. Beth Markle is the clumsier of the two Markle twins. Why do you think this is? Are there certain situations that seem to induce clumsiness more than others?

4. Have you ever found anything like the valuable baseball card that the gang digs up at the end of the story. How much was it worth? Why do we place value on some of these antique items?

5. Draw a picture of a fictional baseball card like the one in chapter nine. Feel free to draw yourself or anyone else you know as the baseball player. Take the exercise one step further and give it away – for free!

NEED MORE HAUNTIQUES?

CHECK OUT THIS
PREVIEW OF...

DARLING DOLL

Hai and I stand outside our school's side entrance. "Casey, you have to go to the disco! You can't turn around and go back home now."

With caution, I eye the familiar brick building. "I don't know," I say. "I really don't feel so good."

Hai groans. "That feeling in your stomach?" Hai says, pointing at my gut. "That's nerves. Think of all the spooky stuff we've seen lately. And *this* is what's going to finally scare you?"

He's right.

Ever since the Markles moved to our small town of Stonewick and opened the Days Gone Buy antique shop, we've got tangled up in a number of paranormal misadventures. In the last two months, I've seen stuff that would scare the pants off of most people. We've encountered a haunted hockey puck, a possessed record player that only played one song and a creepy wagon that rolled through our neighbourhood all on its own.

Sounds random, right? Well, Days Gone Buy used to be Red's General Store, a place that was closed up for decades. When the Markles bought it and fixed it up, they acquired a cellar full of antiques that old Red himself used to collect. So far, three things they've sold from Red's collection had ghosts attached. Somehow we got roped into helping Liz and Beth, the twin Markle daughters, figure out how to help the ghosts move on.

Sure, Hai and I are good guys. But to tell the whole story, Beth Markle is also partly why I'm standing in the car park right now. I've been having second thoughts about going to our first middle school disco. They're calling it the Spring Fever Disco, but I think I've got a fever of my own.

I like Beth. A lot. And I slipped up and told her so just recently. She was nice enough to say she liked me, too. But who knows? Maybe she just likes me as a friend or something. But she *did* hug me.

"Casey?" Hai asks, catching me totally zoning out. "You still there? You look like you've been plugged with a tranquilizer dart."

"I'm fine," I say, shaking it off.

"Good," Hai says. He grabs the sleeve of my jacket and begins tugging at me. "Then let's get inside."

"I still don't know," I say.

"You like Beth, Beth likes you," Hai says. "You said so yourself. What don't you know?"

I'm about to tell him I'm heading back home to spend the night staring at the wall when I hear a familiar voice.

"Hey, Willis! Hey, Boon!"

John Muffleman and a couple of other guys from our class strut up the pavement. They're dressed like they're headed for a disco that's much fancier than advertised. Muffleman even has a tie on.

Last week, I found out John Muffleman likes Beth, too. Muffleman's popular and a nice enough guy, and other than liking the girl I've got my eye on, I really have no problem with him. But imagining Beth as his girlfriend makes my stomach even twistier than it is now.

"Hey, Muffleman," Hai says. "Prom isn't for another few years, man."

"Ha-ha," Muffleman says. "We just want to look good for the ladies."

A minute ago I wanted to go home. Now I want to get inside – fast.

"Good to see you guys," I say. I nod at Hai. "We should probably get in there."

Hai blinks a few times as if he's trying to figure me out and then smiles. "Yeah," he says. "Let's do this, Willis."

I don't think they spent a huge amount of time decorating the cafeteria for the Spring Fever Disco. Music with lots of keyboards, the kind only people my parents' age listen to, plays through two speakers on either side of the room. Mr Harper, our free-spirited music and art teacher by day and our DJ for the night, has set up his laptop. A tiny disco ball throws pinpricks of light that pattern the dance floor and illuminate a couple of handmade signs that have been taped up. I notice that one of them is misspelled: *SPIRNG FEVER.*

My eyes follow the spinning lights to the wall, where almost all of the boys are standing. The girls line the wall on the opposite side of the room. A few adventurous guys are out dancing to some song that sounds like a mix of yodelling, sci-fi sound effects and a drum machine from the 1980s.

A small cluster of girls also huddles out on the dance floor. The only body parts moving are their mouths. They're probably gossiping.

"Where's your girl, Casey?" Hai asks.

"I'm not sure," I say, my stomach bubbling and churning. I'm watching the doorway anytime anyone walks past it.

Mr Harper plays two more songs from bands who've likely broken up decades ago before firing up a slow love song. Immediately, the dance floor completely empties.

"Too bad Beth's not around," Hai says. "This would be the song."

At the doorway, two nearly identical shadows come in from the bright hallway. My heart shifts to fifth gear as Liz and Beth Markle enter the cafeteria.

"Mate," Hai whispers, elbowing my ribs.

"Oh," I say, finding it hard to catch my breath. "Cool."

The Markle twins pause for a second as Liz surveys the room. When she sees the wall where all of the other girls are standing, she drags Beth over. I watch as Beth checks out the rest of the place. Maybe she's looking for me?

"Don't be shy," Mr Harper says. "Get on out and dance, people!" Usually, his voice sounds nasally, but tonight he purrs like a radio guy. "Those walls don't need you to hold 'em up!"

A few people actually head for the floor. I watch Ryan Preston ask Holly Webber to dance. Nick Comstock walks over and gets Sarah Richie off the wall. I can see both Beth and Liz are waiting.

"Do it," Hai whispers. "This is your chance, man."

"I don't know," I say. "I might embarrass her or scare her off."

And now Liz is walking across the cafeteria. At first, I think she's coming over to us. Instead, she gives us a dirty look before marching over to where big Joe Stewell is standing, a few feet to my right.

"Let's go, Joe," Liz says. Joe makes a face like he was dropped in the middle of nowhere. Grabbing him by the arm, Liz tugs Joe onto the dance floor.

The six or seven dancing couples on the floor look a bit uncomfortable. None of them appears to be talking to each other.

They sway back and forth, their hands clamped onto their partners' shoulders and waists as the song's lead singer belts out the soulful refrain.

And now Muffleman steps away from the wall.

"Uh-oh," Hai whispers.

Uncover the mysteries of
HAUNTIQUES...

GHOSTLY GOALIE

Thomas Kingsley Troupe

DARLING DOLL

Thomas Kingsley Troupe

WANDERING WAGON

Thomas Kingsley Troupe

PHANTOM'S FAVOURITE

Thomas Kingsley Troupe